ROAN
WUZ
HERE

JEDI ACADEMY

ATTACK OF THE JOURNAL

by *New York Times* Bestselling author
Jeffrey Brown

and by _____

Scholastic Inc.

This page
is boring . . .

All rights reserved. Published by Scholastic Inc., Publishers since 1920. SCHOLASTIC and associated
logos are trademarks and/or registered trademarks of Scholastic Inc.

The publisher does not have any control over and does not assume any responsibility
for author or third-party websites or their content.

ISBN 978-0-545-85278-4

10 9 8 7 6 5 4 3 2 1   15 16 17 18 19

Printed in the U.S.A.   23
First printing 2015

A long time ago in a galaxy far, far away....

There was a kid named

_____

(that's you) who was destined to write in this book and become the GREATEST Jedi in the GALAXY. Are you ready to have some FUN?! If YES, turn the page. (If NO, close this book, and go eat your veggies.)

Hi, my name's Roan Novachez. I just graduated from Jedi Academy, and soon I'll be a super-awesome Jedi. Being a Jedi is more than just being a lightsaber-wielding knight—it's also keeping the peace throughout the galaxy. It doesn't hurt that you also get to be friends with awesome aliens, build neat-o droids, and fly really cool spaceships!

Heh heh. A Jedi Master, I am. When older you are, what do you want to do?

CREATE AN ALIEN

There are a lot of aliens in this galaxy. If you could create an alien, what would he/she/it look like? How many eyes does it have? What color is its skin? What does it eat? Is it good or bad? Use the space on the next page to draw the alien.

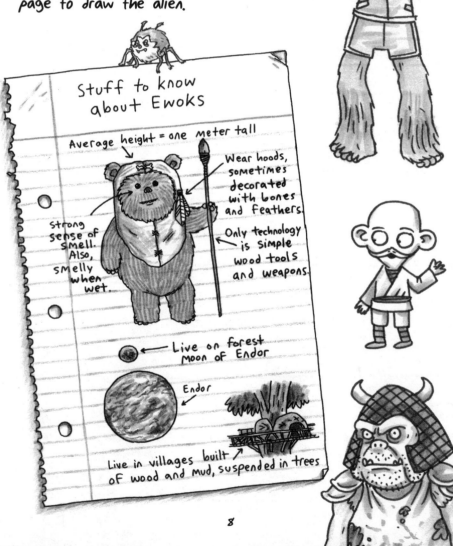

Stuff to know about Ewoks

Average height = one meter tall

Strong sense of smell. Also, smelly when wet.

Wear hoods, sometimes decorated with bones and feathers.

Only technology is simple wood tools and weapons.

Live on forest moon of Endor

Endor

Live in villages built of wood and mud, suspended in trees

BUILD YOUR CLASS SCHEDULE

If you were invited to join Jedi Academy, what kind of classes would you take? Dodgeball? Space-cooking? Lightsaber dueling?

STUDENT: ROAN NOVACHEZ
LEVEL: PADAWAN | SEMESTER: ONE
HOMEROOM: MASTER YODA
CLASS SCHEDULE

0730 - 0850 : BASIC LIFTING WITH THE FORCE
MASTER YODA WILL TEACH STUDENTS TO LIFT THINGS
WITH THE FORCE, INCLUDING ROCKS, DROIDS, AND BOXES

0900 - 0950 : GALACTIC HISTORY
MRS. PILTON WILL TELL STUDENTS HOW THE REPUBLIC
WAS FORMED, WHERE JEDI COME FROM, AND MORE.

1000 - 1050 : ALGEBRA
MRS. PILTON WILL INSTRUCT S
ADVANCED MATH EQUATIONS
USE LATER IN LIFE.

1100 - 1150 : SCIENCE
PRINCIPAL MAR WILL LEAD
NUMEROUS EXPERIMENTS
METHOD.

1200 - 1300 : LUNCH B

1300 - 1350 : ARTS AN
LIBRARIAN LACKBAR W
ESSENTIAL WORKS OF L
ACROSS THE GALAXY.

1400 - 1450 : INTRO. T
MR. GARFIELD WI
BUILD THEIR

1500 - 155
M WIL
Y O

STUDENT: ROAN NOVACHEZ
LEVEL: PADAWAN | SEMESTER: THREE
HOMEROOM: MASTER YODA
CLASS SCHEDULE

0730 - 0850 : ADVANCED USING THE FORCE
MASTER YODA WILL TEACH STUDENTS THE LATEST
AND MOST INTERESTING THINGS TO DO WITH THE FORCE.

0900 - 0950 : HISTORY OF THE JEDI ORDER
MRS. PILTON WILL INSTRUCT STUDENTS ON THE
MOST FAMOUS JEDI MASTERS, EVENTS, AND WARS.

1000 - 1050 : GALACTIC ECOLOGY
PRINCIPAL MAR WILL TEACH STUDENTS ABOUT
VARIOUS PLANETARY ENVIRONMENTS.

: HYPERALGEBRA
WILL MEMORIZE HUNDREDS OF MATH
NS WITH MRS. PILTON.

1300 : LUNCH BREAK

1300 - 1350 : STAR PILOT FLIGHT TRAINING
MR. GARFIELD WILL TRAIN STUDENTS
PILOTING SKILLS, SUCH AS NOT CRAS

1400 - 1450 : PUBLI
LIBRARIAN LACKB
LEARNING TO SP
OF PEOPLE STARI

1500 - 1550 : PHYSIC
STUDENTS WILL BE PUSHED
LIMITS BY KITMUM.

Art class, I like. Paint with my feet, I do.

Hrmph. I like yoga.

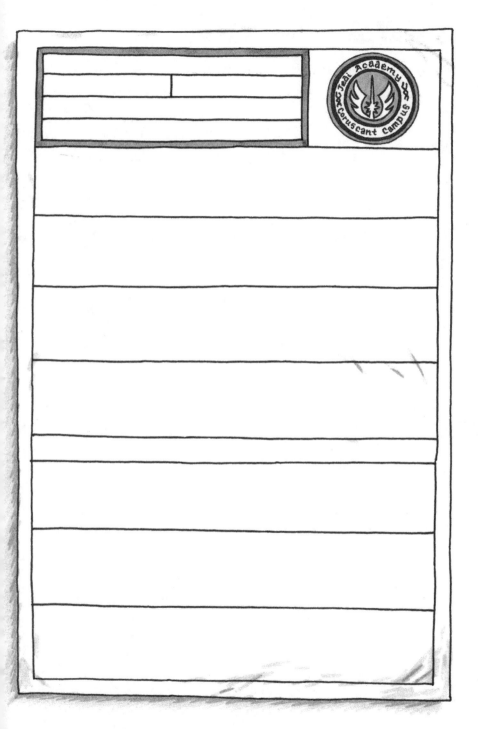

DRAWING 101

Do you like to draw? A good (and easy) way to start drawing people is to use stick figures. You can add life to them with just a few simple strokes. Check out these stick figures battling with lightsabers. Now draw your own.

Hmmm. The Force is strong in your art. Keep drawing, you should.

FINISH THE COMIC

What's happening in this story? It's up to you to write
what everyone is saying...

STORY STARTER

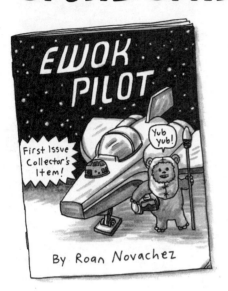

EWOK PILOT

Yub yub!

First Issue Collector's Item!

By Roan Novachez

Roan writes and draws stories about an Ewok Pilot—a furry, funny, and often stubborn Ewok—who (kind of) flies spaceships. If you could write your own space story about a pilot, what would it be about? Here, we'll get you started, and you finish the story . . .

A long time ago, in a galaxy far, far away, there was a young kid who wanted to be a pilot. One day, this kid, named _____ , found a spaceship behind the school. Going inside, the ship seemed to come to life. "Where do you want to go to?" the spaceship asked.
(Now you finish the story!)

_____

_____

_____

_____

_____

_____

_____

_____

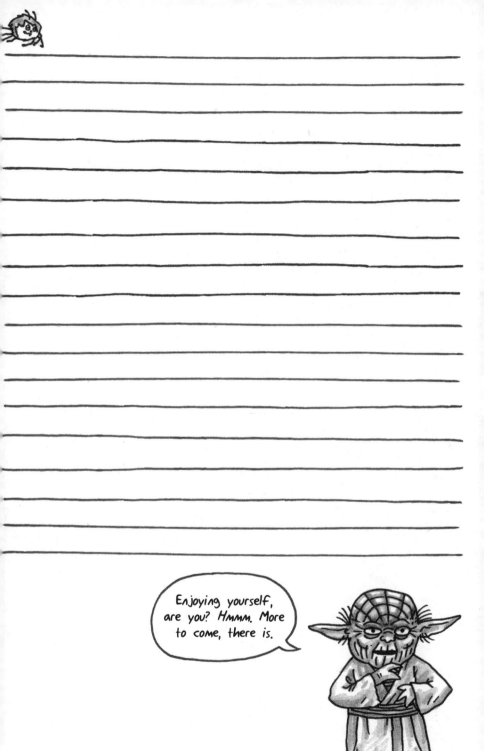

Enjoying yourself, are you? Hmmm. More to come, there is.

15

LISTS

Roan and the other Jedi Academy students got into a huge food fight. Probably because they couldn't stomach Gammy's bizarre cooking. Let's talk about you and food . . . hop!

List five disgusting things to put on a pizza for your worst enemy . . .

_____

What's the WEIRDEST thing you've ever eaten?

_____

What's your favorite food? Would you still eat it if it were covered in _____ ?

_____

What would you rather eat: chocolate-covered grasshoppers or cheese-flavored mealworms?

_____

Did you know on some worlds, insects and eyeballs are considered delicious? Which would you rather eat?

_____

What would you rather do: eat an octopus or be eaten by an alien?

_____

What do you think smells better: tauntaun or rancor?

_____

CREATE YOUR OWN LIGHTSABER

One of the most powerful weapons in the universe belongs to the Jedi—a lightsaber. Each Jedi designs his or her own, choosing a different crystal, color, and look. Describe what kind of lightsaber you want. Would it have one blade or two (like the Sith Lords)? What color would it be? If you don't want a lightsaber, but have another idea for a cool weapon, draw that!

JOURNAL

At the beginning of Roan's story, he was worried about going to PLANT SCHOOL, trying to get into PILOT SCHOOL, and ended up going to JEDI ACADEMY. If you could choose, which school would you go to? And why? Or, if you want, write about one of your adventures at one (or all 3) schools!

_____

_____

_____

_____

Deksh!

MAKE A ROBOT

For a school assignment, Roan and his classmates had to build a robot. Have you ever built a robot? Well, if you haven't, you should try! First though you should make the plans . . . what kind of robot would you create? Would he be made to help you, fight others, or just make pizzas?

LIGHTSABER FENCING
TRAINING DROID

Multiple optical sensors

Shutdown target

Vocal intimidator (will trash-talk you)

parrot perch

360° locomotion system

Adjustable height

bubble gum dispenser

Bells and whistles

Possible Additional Functions:
- Heavy metal drummer
- Flag waver
- Can wash starships?
- Cafeteria dishwasher?
- Practice Soccer goalie

Multiple swivel arms with Kung fu battle grip

23

HOW TO DRAW

I've always loved drawing Ewoks, and I've always loved flying, so it made sense for me to make a comic called EWOK PILOT. Here, I'll show you how to draw Ewok Pilot.

1) First, draw his face. Decide what kind of mood he is in.

2) Draw his "clothes," and add his ears.

3) Then you draw his
   body.

4) Last, you draw
   whatever is
   happening around
   him!

STORY STARTER

Jedi have all kinds of amazing abilities. They can use the Force to move or "push" things with their minds. They can jump high into the air. They can use Jedi mind tricks to persuade the weak-minded. They have lightsabers. And Sith Lords can create Force-lightning! If you could have any Force power, what would it be? Write a story about how you discover your power and what you would do with it.

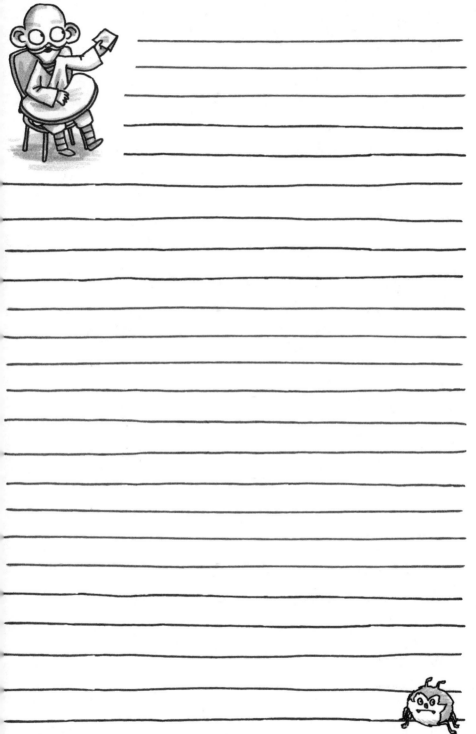

FINISH THE STORY

Reg and Jax grew up on Tatooine, just like Roan. But they went to Pilot School and have been flying all over the universe. They think they're pretty cool—though actually, they ARE pretty cool. But they're having a hard time finishing their story. Fill in the blanks with your own words to help them out.

Reg and Jax always wanted to be the

_____ star pilots in

the galaxy. One day, they decided to borrow the

_____ and use it to fly

to the planet _____.

But on their way, a bunch of bad guys called the

_____ came after them,

wanting to steal their lunch money.

Reg and Jax forgot to arm their weapons, so they
had to lose the bad guys. First, they flew into an
asteroid belt. But when they tried to land, a giant

_____ came out of a

hole and tried to _____

them. Finally, they lost the bad guys. But then a bunch
of space pirates came after them, wanting to take
their _____.

They punched in the hyperdrive and zipped away.

They finally got to their destination, but once they
were there, they were attacked by hundreds of female

_____ who wanted to

cook them in their _____.

Reg and Jax had to get out of there fast! And they
did. But that's a story for another day . . .

YODA, SPEAK LIKE!

Speak backward, some people think I do. But maybe, speak backward, it's other people who do. Hmmm. Hehehe.
Try and speak like me, you should.

Actually. Do or do not. There is no try.

Things Yoda Said This Week

calm

at peace

(maybe Yoda is wrinkly from spending lots of time relaxing in hot baths!)

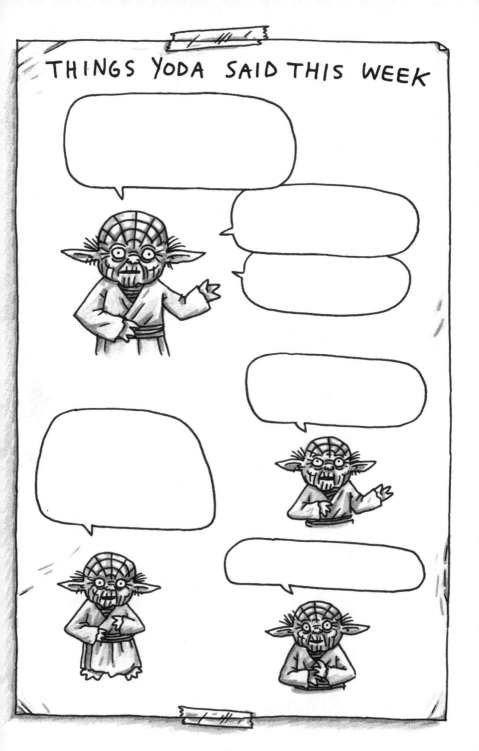

DRAW YOUR FRIENDS AS ALIENS

What if you and your friends were from different planets? What would you (and they) look like? Draw your friends as aliens. Or your parents. Or even your teachers!

INVENT A SECRET HANDSHAKE

Do you and your friends have a secret handshake? All cool people should have a secret handshake. I have, like, two hundred of them. (I just wish I had more friends to use them with . . .)

Describe your secret handshake here . . . then practice with your best friend.

JOKE TIME

Why did the angry Jedi cross the road?

To get to the dark side!

What do you call a potato that has gone to the dark side?

Vader tots!

When did Yoda suspect the evil chancellor was turning to the dark side?

In the Sith grade.

Why is a droid mechanic never lonely?

Because he's always MAKING new friends.

Why did Yoda visit the bank?

He needed a bank clone!

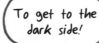

JOURNAL

Roan has an older brother and a younger brother. Dav likes to joke around with Roan, but he also gives him good advice. And Ollie looks up to Roan, and wants to be just like him when he gets older. Do you look up to anybody? Do you have anyone who looks up to you?

37

SPORTS AND STUFF

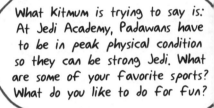

RRRRRAAAARRRGGHHH!!!

What Kitmum is trying to say is:
At Jedi Academy, Padawans have
to be in peak physical condition
so they can be strong Jedi. What
are some of your favorite sports?
What do you like to do for fun?

Ugh. Sports are too much work for
me ... no, thanks. I like video games.
What are some of your things to do
for fun that don't involve running
around and sweating?

Hey!

AAAUUGGHH!

STORY STARTER

Telling spooky stories around a campfire is a tradition all around the galaxy. What's the scariest story you've ever heard? Or maybe just write your own here with the space provided.

_____

_____

_____

_____

_____

Even I think that's scary.

ALIEN PETS

Roan and Gaiana cared for a furry little voorpak from Naboo. The galaxy is filled with all kinds of weird animals and creatures and stuff. If you could have any pet alien, what would it be? What kind of adventures (and trouble) would you and your new pet get into? Write a story about it . . .

webweaver

katarn

I would get a baby rancor. Then I'd train it to eat everyone. Well, everyone except me.

MORE JOKES

Uh-oh, looks like Ronald and Cronah are at it again. Do you know any jokes? If so, write 'em down!

How do Ewoks talk over far distances?

E-Walkie talkies.

Which side of an Ewok has the most hair?

The outside!

What does Jabba the Hutt eat?

Hutt dogs!

How do you unlock a door on Kashyyyk?

With a Wook-key.

What is a Jedi's favorite toy?

A Yo-Yoda.

What do you call a man who brings dinner to a rancor?

The appetizer.

I prefer poetry:
Roses are red
Violets are blue
If you love Jedi
May the Force be with you.

45

STORY STARTER

It's time to write another story. I'll get you started, and then YOU finish it!

The giant robot sat up and looked around. He couldn't remember who he was or who made him. He wasn't even sure if he was a good guy or a bad guy. As he looked around the strange spaceship, he wondered where he was and how he got here. He took a step off the metal table and stood up. He was dizzy for just a moment and then everything shook violently for one second. Then everything was still. Then he realized why. The spaceship had landed. The door opened automatically. The first thing he saw was nothing but light, but then . . .

_____

_____

_____

_____

_____

_____

_____

_____

47

SELF-PORTRAIT

When Roan was drawing, he created several different versions of Yoda. Some of these could be called different styles of art. There's no right or wrong way to draw something, just different ones! Why don't you use the space provided to draw YOURSELF? Use a photo or a mirror, and then draw yourself in cartoon form. Remember, there's no right or wrong way to do it—just have fun!

JOURNAL

It wasn't easy for Roan to become an awesome Jedi. It took a lot of work. He had to deal with homework and friends and bullies and all kinds of crazy stuff—and at the same time, he had to read, train, and listen to his teachers. What's something in your life that you have had to practice so you can become better?

Yeha!

FINISH THE COMIC

What are they saying?
I don't know. You write their dialogue.

This is a free page.
Do something awesome.

VIDEO GAMES

What are some of your favorite video games?
If you could create you own video game, what would it
be about? Would it have dragons or monsters or aliens?
Who would be the hero? Would there be weapons or
mazes? What would it be called? Write or draw about
your dream video game here.

MAZES AND LABYRINTHS

Obstacle courses and mazes are fun to do and fun to make! Design your own maze or obstacle course on the next page.

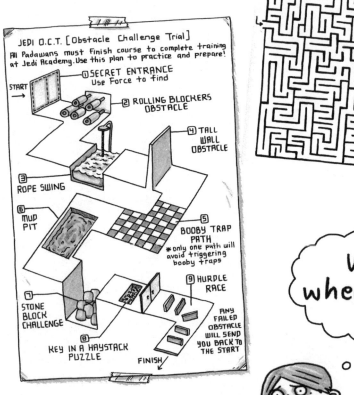

JEDI O.C.T. [Obstacle Challenge Trial]
All Padawans must finish course to complete training at Jedi Academy. Use this plan to practice and prepare!

START →

1 SECRET ENTRANCE
Use Force to find

2 ROLLING BLOCKERS OBSTACLE

4 TALL WALL OBSTACLE

3 ROPE SWING

6 MUD PIT

5 BOOBY TRAP PATH
*only one path will avoid triggering booby traps

9 HURDLE RACE

7 STONE BLOCK CHALLENGE

ANY FAILED OBSTACLE WILL SEND YOU BACK TO THE START

KEY IN A HAYSTACK PUZZLE

FINISH →

Wait, where am I?

56

WHAT'S GOING ON IN YOUR BRAIN?!

Roan has a LOT going on in his brain every hour that he's awake (and even when he's trying to sleep). What's going on in your brain? What do you think about the most and the least? Make a list or draw a picture like Roan's.

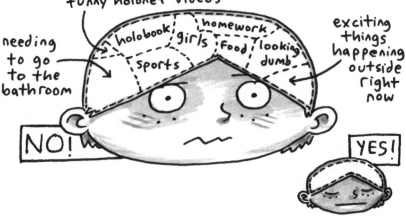

2. Clear your mind of thoughts

funny holonet videos

needing to go to the bathroom

holobook

sports

girls

homework

Food

looking dumb

exciting things happening outside right now

NO!

YES!

Write a fake article about yourself in the Jedi Academy student newspaper. Make sure to draw pictures!

CAMPAIGN POSTER

If you ran for president of the galaxy, what would your campaign poster say and look like? Draw one here.

DESIGN YOUR OWN SPACESHIP

There are all kinds of cool spaceships out in space. Ewok Pilot and Jawa Pilot both have ships (or at least they did, but they keep blowing them up!). And Roan has always wanted to be a star pilot (although Mr. G. is always making him wash ships instead of fly them). If you could be a star pilot and design your own spaceship, what would it look like? Make some sketches here!

MAPS

Drawing maps is awesome. Here's a map to Pasha's house. Now you draw a map to somewhere! Maybe to school? Or a friend's house? If you can't think of a real place to draw a map, then make something up. Maybe a treasure map. Treasure is awesome, too.

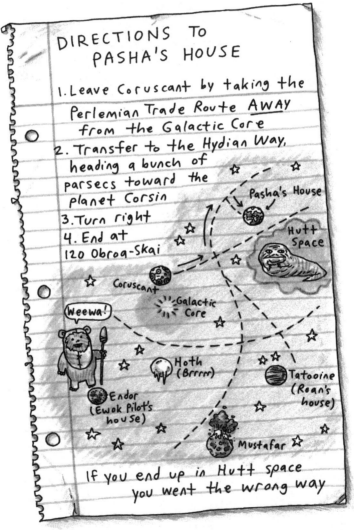

DIRECTIONS TO
PASHA'S HOUSE

1. Leave Coruscant by taking the Perlemian Trade Route AWAY from the Galactic Core
2. Transfer to the Hydian Way, heading a bunch of parsecs toward the planet Corsin
3. Turn right
4. End at 120 Obroa-Skai

Pasha's House

Hutt Space

Coruscant

Galactic Core

Weewa!

Hoth (Brrrrr)

Tatooine (Roan's house)

Endor (Ewok Pilot's house)

Mustafar

If you end up in Hutt space you went the wrong way

67

NAPTIME

Looks like everyone fell asleep. Do whatever you want with this free space.

JOURNAL

If you were in Roan's class, who would you hang out with? Who would be your best friend? Who would be your enemy? Who would be your favorite teacher?

71

VACATIONS

Roan grew up on the desert planet Tatooine. Then he went to Coruscant, a planet that is one huge city, to attend Jedi Academy. He even visited the ice planet Hoth. What are some of the coolest (or warmest) places you've been to? What is the most remote? What is the most populated? What is the highest place you've been to? Lowest? Draw some pictures of the places you've been!

STORY STARTER

Imagine you went to Jedi Academy. Write a story about your day there. What would it be like? What kind of trouble would you get into? What kind of fun would you have?

LISTS

If you could have a space adventure with people you know, whom would you take? Below are some spaces to fill in the people you know as space heroes (and villains)!

FIST BUMP WITH THE FORCE!

PILOT: _____

COPILOT: _____

JEDI: _____

JEDI MASTER: _____

JEDI PADAWAN: _____

SITH LORD: _____

SIDEKICK: _____

PRINCESS: _____

DROIDS: _____

STORY STARTER

Now write a story with the cast you created. Make
sure you have fun adventures!

_____

_____

_____

_____

_____

_____

_____

_____

_____

_____

_____

_____

_____

_____

_____

_____

_____

_____

JOURNAL

Roan isn't a fan of bugs. Is there anything you don't like? What are you most afraid of? Don't be embarrassed, even Jedi are afraid of stuff. But they must learn to overcome their fear.

FACE DOODLES

Do you ever doodle on top of pictures? What about adding a moustache or a pair of glasses? Maybe some fangs or a funny hairdo? It's easy and fun. You try it now.

PARTY TIME!

Roan has been to lots of school dances, ice cream socials, and other kinds of parties. Kids (and aliens) like to party. If you could throw a party, what would be the theme? What kind of music would you play? Who would you invite? What would make it the coolest party ever?

PADAWAN OBSERVER

Write another fake article in the Jedi Academy student newspaper. It can be about whatever you want. Have fun with it!

OLLIE'S PAGES

Roan not here.
This my page now.
I draw somthin.
OLLie!

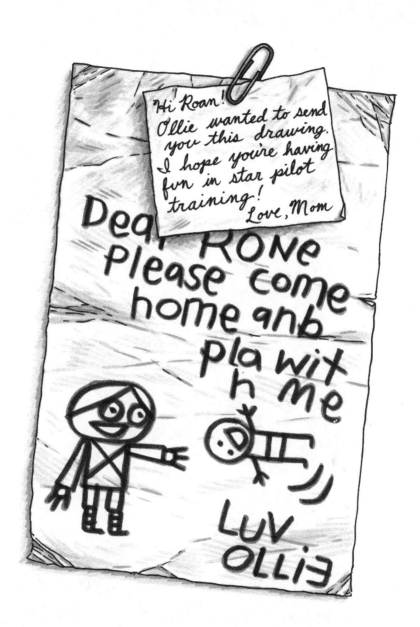

ANIMAL DRAWING

The galaxy is filled with all kinds of wild animals. What's the coolest/weirdest/craziest animal you've seen in real life? Practice drawing it here.

STORY STARTER

Imagine you crash-landed on a strange alien planet . . . now write a story about it! Who would you meet? What would you do? How would you escape?

_____

_____

_____

_____

_____

_____

_____

_____

_____

_____

93

TEACHERS

Who is your favorite teacher at school? Who is the hardest? Write a little bit about your teachers or draw a picture of them. If you don't want to do that, then pick a teacher from Jedi Academy!

WRITE YOUR OWN STORY

All right, here is your final test . . . Time to write your own story from scratch! You decide what happens and who the characters are!

May the Force be with you.

DRAW YOUR OWN COMIC

Time to make your own comic. There's nothing but empty panels for you to fill in with your own art, balloons, and story. Can't wait to see what you make!

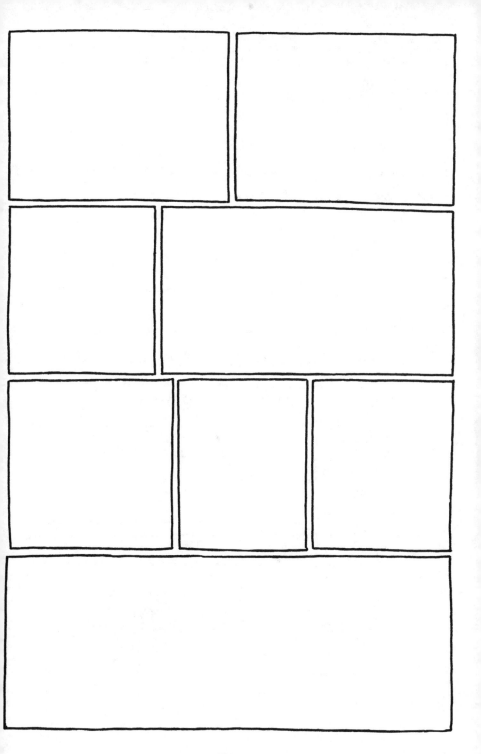

END-OF-THE-YEAR AWARDS

It's almost the end . . . I know, too bad, so sad. But make sure to fill in some of the people who inspired this book. Your friends, your family, maybe even people you don't like all that much. Then say what they're good for (or bad at)!

The Padawan Observer End-of-the-Year Awards!

Best Student

Highest Flying

Most Rhythmic

Greenest

Eedada huutaveet!

VORPEE CLONE REVEAL

I guess you figured out by now that Voorpee got cloned again. Voorpaks are all over this book.

But can you count them? Go through and find every Voorpee clone. There should be _____ of them.

Answer: 41

DIPLOMA

Write your name here. You graduated!

Jedi Academy

Jedi Academy Coruscant Campus

This certifies that

has completed the Padawan Course of study prescribed by the Jedi Council of the planet Coruscant and is therefore entitled to this

Diploma

In Testimony whereof, we have here unto affixed our signatures.

PRINCIPAL MAR

Master Yoda   Principal

Homeroom Instructor

MR. GARFIELD

Jedi Mentor

EWOK DICTIONARY

Ewok Pilot says some pretty hilarious stuff, doesn't he? What's that? What do you mean you don't speak Ewok?! Well, let's help you out . . . Here's some translations for you. Now you can go back through this book and translate the crazy stuff that Ewok Pilot is saying!

Acha — okay, all right

Ah-ah — water

Allayloo — celebrate

Ando — forward

Azar — magic

Bi toto — direction

Bok chuu-ock — far away

Bugdoo — hungry

Cha — them

Chaaa — this one

Chak — yes

Che womok! — Beware!

Chek — soup

Choo doo — enough

Dangar — attack

Danthee — maybe

Deksh — oh, dear/oh, my

Den — no

Drik — happy

Ee chee wa maa! — Wow, gee whiz! Oh my goodness!

Ee choya — hey

Eedada huutaveet — spaceship

Ees — we

Ehda — evil, or bad

Eyok-nee-chug — What is that?

Fudana — wait

Geetch — push

Glek — sad

Goopa — hi

Goot — good

Grenchicit — hang on/hold on

Gunda — yummy

Gyeesh — please

Ileeay — stop

Jeerota — friend

Kaiya — giddy up!

Kush drojh? — What's going on?

Labu labu — how much?

Luka — stars

Luu — beautiful

Manna manna — food

Na-chin — tribe

Na goo — stop!

Nuv — love

Ooba — rain

Reh rehluu — dance

Roda — to eat

Sku — hello

Sunee — sun

Teeha — thank you

T'hesh — quiet

Thuk — rock

Toto — is/does

Treek — go

Tyeht danti? — What happened?

Tyehtgeethin — stranger

Uuta — sky

Weewa — home

Yaa-yaah! — Greetings

Yeha — good-bye

Yub nub — freedom

Yub yub — Let's go

Yubnub — hooray

Zeekee — safe

JAWA DICTIONARY

You don't speak Jawa, either?! It's like you're not even from this galaxy. Here, I'll help you out with a dictionary of Jawa translations, too. Make sure you go back through <u>Jedi Academy</u>, <u>Return of the Padawan</u>, and <u>The Phantom Bully</u>, and translate all the hilarious comics featuring Ewok Pilot and his best Jawa friend.

Ashuna — go
Ayafa — clan
Baba — days
Bazzok — cook
Bok — far
Bom'loo — bargain
Chikua — them
Dooka — junk
Eyta — friend
Gogowa — run
Gomjam — always
Ha'mfoo — burn
Hunya — enemy
Ibana — yes
Ikee — I
Ja-bo-ba — Jedi
Jubinloo — city

Kiizci — cave
Ko lopo — broken
Kurruzza — repair
Lopima — stars
Mambay — okay
M'tuske — steal
M'um m'aloo — greetings, hello
Neta — no
Okka — up
Oko — cold
Opakwa — spare parts
Ratapa — knife
Reve — ship
Rubac — rust
Sabioto — stop
Shanay — sleep

Shootogawa — shoot, blast
Sooga — food
Taa baa — thank you
Tando — fix
Theek — run
Toineepa — credit
Ton ton — sand
Ubanya — good day, good-bye
Umka — walk
Utinni — Wow! Come here. Also, a common battle cry.
Waff-mla — dessert
Wass — hot
Ysas — equal
Yuyu — right

Here are some common Jawa phrases:

Utto nye usabia atoonyoba? — Want to buy used droid?

A beton nya mombay m'bwa! — This is mine, all mine!

Ookwas dok pundwa keena? — Where is the nearest fuel station?

Etee uwanna waa. — I want to trade.

ABOUT THE AUTHOR
(THAT'S YOU!)

This is the part where you say something cool about yourself. Imagine if you had to sum yourself up in 2-3 sentences, what would you say? Draw yourself if you want, too. For inspiration, look at the last page of the Jedi Academy books and see how Jeffrey Brown did it.

Heh Heh Heh